E   c.1

Holl, Adelaide
The rain puddle

DEC 0 6 ...

	DATE DUE		
	OVERDUE FINE $1/day		

THE RAIN PUDDLE

by Adelaide Holl

pictures by Roger Duvoisin

LOTHROP, LEE & SHEPARD CO., NEW YORK

8 9 10 75

 L.C.C. No.: 65-22026. Printed in U.S.A.

Plump hen was picking and pecking in the meadow grass.

"Cluck, cluck! Cluck, cluck!" she said softly to herself.

All at once, she came to a rain puddle.

"Dear me!" she cried. "A plump little hen has fallen into the water!"

And away she ran calling, "Awk, awk! Cut-a-cut! Cut-a-cut! Cut-a-cut!"

Turkey was eating corn in the barnyard.

"Come at once!" called plump hen. "A hen is in the rain puddle!"

Away went turkey to see for himself.

"Gobble-obble-obble!" he cried when he looked in. "It is not a plump hen. It is a big, bright turkey gobbler!"

Pig was crunching red apples in the orchard. He heard the news. Off he waddled to take a look.

"Snort, snort! Oink, oink! They are both wrong," pig said to himself. "It is a beautiful, fat pig that has fallen into the rain puddle. I must get help at once!"

Curly sheep was nibbling sweet clover in the pasture, and cow was softly chewing her cud under a shady tree.

"What is going on?" they said to one another. "Let us go and see."

They found all the other animals crowded around the puddle together.

"A whole barnyard full of animals has fallen into the water," they all exclaimed. "We must run for help!"

While all the animals were running about in great excitement, the sun came out. The sun shone warm and bright. It dried the rain puddle all up.

Plump hen stopped running around in circles and cried, "Awk, awk! Cut, cut! Look! The animals have all climbed out safely!"

And away she went to pick and peck in the meadow grass.

"Gobble-obble-obble! So they have!" agreed turkey. And off he went to eat corn in the barnyard.

"You are quite right," snorted pig. And he waddled off to crunch red apples in the orchard.

Curly sheep said, "Baaaa, baaaa," and went back to nibble sweet clover in the pasture.

"Moooo, moooo!" said cow. "All of the animals escaped!" And off she went to find a shady tree and to chew her cud.

Wise old owl looked down from a tree above and chuckled to himself.

The Rain Puddle
was photoset in 20 point Times Roman, by Wescott and Thompson, Inc.,
and bound by The Book Press, Brattleboro, Vermont